D0359908

DELPHINE PERRET

A BEAR NAMED

BJORN

TRANSLATED BY ANTONY SHUGAAR

GECKO PRESS

CONTENTS

PAGE 01
THE SOFA

PAGE 09
THE CARNIVAL

PAGE 19
NOTHING

PAGE 27
THE PRESENT

PAGE 37
GLASSES

PAGE 45
IT'S TIME

THE SOFA

BJORN LIVES IN A CAVE.
THE WALLS ARE VERY SMOOTH.
THE FLOOR IS PRETTY COMFORTABLE.

AND RIGHT IN FRONT OF THE CAVE
HE HAS TENDER GREEN GRASS AND
A ROUGH-BARKED TREE, PERFECT FOR
SCRATCHING HIS BACK.

BJORN ALSO HAS A
MAILBOX WHERE LETTERS
SOMETIMES ARRIVE.

LIKE, FOR EXAMPLE, THE FLUORESCENT PAGE,
DELIVERED JUST THIS MORNING, ANNOUNCING
IN CAPITAL LETTERS: "CONGRATULATIONS!"

BJORN READS ON.

HE LEARNS HE'S BEEN SELECTED.
HE HAS WON A PLUMP
THREE-SEATER SOFA, AND
THIS WILL CHANGE HIS LIFE
AND MAKE HIM VERY HAPPY.

That very afternoon, a delivery
truck pulls up outside Bjorn's cave.
Two people unload a large red sofa.
They set it down inside the cave,
tip their caps and leave.

Then the rabbit hops over.
"What's that?" she asks.
"It's a sofa," Bjorn says,
a little embarrassed.

BJORN SITS DOWN. IT'S SOFT. OKAY, NOT BAD.
THE RABBIT WANTS TO TRY IT, TOO.
YES, NICE AND SOFT. SHE LIKES IT.

THE BADGER DROPS BY AND SETTLES IN.
THE SQUIRREL HAS ALREADY TOLD THE WHOLE
FOREST. THE WEASEL SPRAWLS OUT, THE FOX
CURLS UP. QUITE THE EVENT, THIS NEW SOFA.

"You're lucky, Bjorn.
It's great having a sofa,"
says the rabbit,
draping herself over
the back of it.

Bjorn isn't sure. Actually, he thinks
this sofa is too soft. And it takes up
the whole cave.

He no longer has a corner for sleeping.
Or a corner for eating.

BJORN LOOKS PRETTY UNHAPPY, TO TELL THE TRUTH.
THE CHICKADEE NOTICES.

"BJORN, ARE YOU GOING TO KEEP THE SOFA?"
"UM, SURE, IT'S GREAT TO HAVE A SOFA."
"REALLY?"
"EVERYBODY SEEMS TO THINK SO..."
"HMM, BUT YOU? DO YOU THINK IT'S GREAT?"
"UM...NO," BJORN ADMITS.

HE CLEARS HIS THROAT AND ANNOUNCES:
"ACTUALLY, I'M GIVING THIS SOFA AWAY.
WHO WANTS IT?"
THE RABBIT LEAPS UP: "LET'S PUT IT
OUTSIDE FOR EVERYONE TO USE!"
"GOOD IDEA," SAYS BJORN.

THEY PUT THE SOFA IN THE SMALL
CLEARING WITH THE THREE OAK TREES.

THE WEASEL DECLARES: "THERE YOU ARE!
AFTER A BIT OF RAIN, IT WILL SMELL WONDERFULLY MOSSY!"

IN THE LATE AFTERNOON LIGHT, EVERYONE IS DELIGHTED
WITH THE WOODLAND SOFA.

BJORN THINKS OF HIS
CAVE, NOW WITHOUT
A SOFA, AND IS HAPPY.

The Carnival

Bjorn likes reading.
Sometimes he finds clothing
catalogues in his mailbox.

Sometimes he comes upon them by chance.

BJORN OFTEN LEAFS
THROUGH THESE
CATALOGUES WITH THE FOX.
THEY FIND THEM REALLY INTERESTING.

SOME HUMANS LOOK VERY MYSTERIOUS. OTHERS SMILE,
BARING ALL THEIR TEETH. THEY PAINT THEIR EYES,
PROUDLY SHOW OFF THEIR MUSCLES AND,
NO MATTER WHERE THEY ARE, FIND WIND TO
TOSS THEIR HAIR ABOUT.

Today, while Bjorn is deep
in his reading, the fox has
a brilliant idea.

"What if we dress up
as humans? What if
we have...a carnival!"

Bjorn loves this idea.
He starts a list, just thinking aloud:

"We'll need clothes, something to paint
our eyes with, and a few thingamajigs
to put in our hair."

THE FOX KNOWS WHERE TO FIND CERTAIN ITEMS.
THE MAGPIE HAS A TREASURE COLLECTION. FOR THE REST,
HIKERS TEND TO DROP THINGS ALONG THE WAY.

IT'S A GOOD START.

BESIDE THE TENT OF SOME CAMPERS WHO'VE GONE WALKING
IN THE FOREST, THEY FIND CLOTHES DRYING ON A LINE.

EVERYTHING THEY NEED: TROUSERS, UNDERWEAR, SHIRTS,
A SCARF, AND EVEN A CAP WITH A JAM STAIN.

THE WEASEL FINDS SANDALS UNDER A BENCH.

THEIR ARMS FULL OF TREASURES,
THEY HEAD HOME AND SET TO WORK.

THE FOX, WHO'S HAD A RADIO FOR YEARS,
PLUGS IN THE SPEAKERS AND UNROLLS
A CARPET IN THE MIDDLE OF THE CLEARING.

At seven o'clock sharp, everyone turns up
in disguise with something to share:
hazelnuts,
a tart with blueberries
—or fleas.

It's the finest carnival of pretend humans ever
seen in the forest. The festivities go on until late.

THE WEASEL SHOWS OFF HER DANCING, AND THE
BADGER SINGS BADLY OUT OF TUNE BUT SO HAPPILY
THAT NO ONE HAS THE HEART TO CRITICIZE.

THEY DO THE CONGA AND THEY DANCE THE TWIST.

THEY SWAP DISGUISES. WHEN IT'S TIME TO GO,
THEY'RE BETTER FRIENDS THAN EVER.

EARLY THE NEXT MORNING, THEY RETURN
THE CLOTHES TO THEIR RIGHTFUL OWNERS
WITH A THANK-YOU NOTE. THE FOREST PEOPLE
LIKE TO SHOW JUST HOW CIVILIZED THEY ARE.

NOTHING

NOT MUCH HAPPENS IN A BEAR'S LIFE.

OFTEN BJORN DOES NOTHING AT ALL.
BUT HE'S NEVER BORED.

He might happen to be sitting
on a nice warm rock
or a patch of mossy grass
and someone comes by.
Maybe the squirrel.

"What are you doing, Bjorn?"
"I'm watching the trees grow."
"But you can't see anything!"
"You can see the leaves."
"But they don't grow!"
"Give them time."

And he goes on watching.

Then he yawns so loudly that the chickadee
thinks she can hear the wind springing up.

THE RABBIT BRINGS HIM THE
LATEST NEWS. IF THEY'RE
IN THE MOOD TO PLAY,
SHE'LL GET OUT HER CARDS
AND DEAL.

THE RABBIT WINS EVERY HAND
BUT FINISHES WITH CARD TRICKS
TO MAKE UP FOR IT.

THEY HEAR DUCKS IN THE DISTANCE.
IT MUST BE DINNER TIME.

BJORN SITS AT A STUMP TO EAT.
OR HE JUST PLOPS DOWN ON
THE GRASS FOR HIS MEAL.

THEN HE ROLLS IN THE DUST
AND SHAKES OUT HIS COAT.

HE TAKES A QUIET NAP IN
THE SILENCE BESIDE THE BADGER.

SOMETIMES HE BUMPS AGAINST THE TREE
AND MAKES AN APPLE FALL. SINCE IT'S THERE,
HE BITES INTO IT.

THE BADGER GNAWS AT HIS FLEAS
AND BJORN WATCHES, TELLING
HIMSELF HE'LL DO THE SAME.
ONCE HE'S FINISHED RESTING.

BUT WHEN HIS NAP IS OVER, HE IS TAKEN
BY A SUDDEN CRAVING FOR HONEY.
HE KNOWS WHERE THERE'S SOME HONEYCOMB.

SOMETIMES HE READS.
ALONE, OR WITH THE FOX FOR COMPANY.

HE AND THE SQUIRREL SOMETIMES
DRAW IN HALF-DRY MUD.

HE LOOKS AT CATERPILLARS.

CATCHES A CRUNCHY FLY.

THEN HE GOES HOME. IF HE AND THE WEASEL CROSS PATHS,
THEY'LL SHARE SOME QUAIL EGGS. IF THE WEATHER IS NICE,
THEY'LL COUNT STARS.

THE DAY IS DONE.
BJORN CAN'T WAIT
TO START OVER
AGAIN TOMORROW.

THE PRESENT

RAMONA IS ONE OF BJORN'S FRIENDS,
THE ONLY ONE WHO DOESN'T LIVE IN
THE FOREST. SHE GOES TO SCHOOL.
AND THAT TAKES UP MOST OF HER TIME.

SOMETIMES THE SCHOOL
GOES ON A FIELD TRIP.
THE CHILDREN TRAVEL BY BUS,
BRINGING BOOTS AND POTATO CHIPS.
THEY WALK INTO THE FOREST
TWO BY TWO, HOLDING HANDS.

THAT'S HOW RAMONA
MET BJORN.

A FEW DAYS AGO,
RAMONA SENT A PRESENT:
A FORK. BJORN KNOWS
EXACTLY HOW TO USE IT.

HE WALKS BACK AND
FORTH WITH HIS FORK.
IT'S BRAND NEW. AND SHINY.

THE FOX ASKS WHAT IT'S FOR.
BJORN SHOWS HIM. IT'S A DELIGHT.
IT SCRATCHES BETTER THAN THE
ROUGHEST BARK ON THE ROUGHEST
TREE TRUNK.

ALL OF HIS FRIENDS THINK
BJORN IS VERY LUCKY TO HAVE
RECEIVED SUCH A GIFT.

"BJORN, YOU SHOULD SEND HER
A PRESENT, TOO!"

THAT'S TRUE. BUT WHAT? IT'S NOT
EASY TO CHOOSE A GOOD GIFT.

BJORN REMEMBERS A PLACE IN THE RIVER WHERE
THE STONES ARE ALL ROUND.

PAWS IN THE WATER, HE
GATHERS THE SMOOTHEST
ONES HE CAN FIND.

IT'S NICE, HAVING A ROUND STONE TO KEEP IN YOUR POCKET.
BUT CHILDREN HAVE SMALL CLOTHES WITH SMALL POCKETS.
"SHE'LL ONLY LOSE THIS PERFECT PEBBLE," BJORN TELLS
HIMSELF. HE THROWS IT BACK INTO THE RIVER, WHERE IT
HITS A PASSING TROUT.

BJORN PICKS A
PRETTY POPPY.

BUT BY THE TIME HE'S HOME, IT'S A CRUMPLED
SCRAP IN HIS CLAWS.

AHA, HE'S GOT IT!
HE KNOWS WHERE TO FIND WILD HONEY!
NOW THAT'S A FINE PRESENT!

But when he gets back, with a new bee sting on the top of his head, he realizes that this sticky gift will never fit into an envelope. Much less come out of it.

What on earth can he give her?

Just then, a seed lands on the tip of his nose.

Of course! A seed! Everyone agrees. It's the perfect gift.

EACH ONE PUTS A SEED
THEY'VE FOUND INTO
A LITTLE ENVELOPE.

BJORN MAILS THE LETTER.

Everyone is very excited because none of them knows what will grow from their seed. That evening, they fall asleep thinking about what will become of those seeds, down there in Ramona's town.

Glasses

Today there will be medical
check-ups in the forest.

That's another
one of the
owl's ideas

Sometimes the owl might suddenly
decide to throw a cockroach party
or make them spend a whole morning
on housework. They go along with him
because they like the way he looks
after them all.

And once a year he makes up his mind
that it's time for their check-ups.

He checks them for fleas.

For dirty teeth.

For good, strong breathing.

One time, Bjorn swallowed
a mosquito that way.
When taking a deep
breath for the owl.

THE OWL ALSO CHECKS THEIR SENSE OF SMELL.
IS THAT A FAINT WHIFF OF FUNGUS? OF EARTH?
OF VIOLETS?

BJORN ALWAYS GETS VERY GOOD GRADES FOR SMELLING.
HE HAS AN EXCEPTIONAL SNOUT. AND THEN IT'S TIME
TO CHECK EVERYONE'S VISION.

HOW MANY
APPLES ON THAT
TREE BACK THERE?

WHAT KIND OF CATERPILLAR IS CLINGING TO THAT LEAF?
CAN YOU SEE ANYTHING ON THAT HILL?

TODAY BJORN THINKS HE'S DONE
A GOOD JOB OF ANSWERING,
JUST LIKE HIS FRIENDS. AS USUAL.

BUT HE COUNTED TWELVE APPLES
WHEN THERE WERE ONLY NINE,
DIDN'T SEE THE TREES ON THE HILL,
AND WAS WRONG ABOUT THE CATERPILLAR.

TO THE OWL, IT'S CLEAR:
BJORN IS THOROUGHLY SHORTSIGHTED.

"SHORTSIGHTED AS A MOLE?"
BJORN WONDERS, THINKING
ABOUT HIS FRIEND.

HE URGENTLY NEEDS TO
FIND GLASSES.

THE MAGPIE RUMMAGES THROUGH
HER TREASURES AND FISHES OUT
THREE PAIRS: A NICE GREEN PAIR,
ONE MADE OF TORTOISESHELL,
AND A HEAVY PAIR WITH STRIPES.

THE FIRST PAIR IS TOO NARROW.
THE SECOND MAKES BJORN SQUINT.
THE THIRD SEEMS FINE.
BJORN COUNTS NINE APPLES AND
RECOGNIZES THE CATERPILLAR.

EVERYONE ADMIRES BJORN'S GLASSES
AND HOW SERIOUS THEY MAKE HIM LOOK.

THE OWL IS SATISFIED WITH HOW THAT TURNED OUT.
"VERY GOOD," HE SAYS, "THAT'S THAT TAKEN CARE OF!"
AND HE GOES BACK TO CHECKING THE WEASEL'S
YELLOWISH TEETH.

BJORN THANKS HIM AND GOES HOME.
HE HANGS HIS GLASSES ON A BRANCH.

ALL THINGS CONSIDERED,
HE'D RATHER SEE THE WORLD
BLURRED. HE'LL KEEP HIS
GLASSES FOR SPECIAL OCCASIONS.

It's Time

REALLY? IT'S THAT TIME? THIS MORNING
THERE'S A CHANGE IN THE AIR.
YOU CAN SMELL IT IN THE LEAVES
PILING UP AT THE FOOT OF THE TREES,
IN THE FAINT WHIFF OF MUSHROOMS.
THAT'S IT, THE SAME AS EVERY YEAR.

EXCEPT, NOT EXACTLY.

BJORN HAS THE FEELING THAT IT'S TIME.

WHEN HE RUNS INTO THE FOX, THOUGH,
HE'S HESITANT.
"DO YOU SENSE A CHANGE IN THE AIR?"
"SURE, A LITTLE."
"IT'S TIME, ISN'T IT?"
"I DON'T KNOW. I HAVE TO GET GOING."

BJORN IS STILL UNSURE
WHEN HE COMES ACROSS THE ANTS.
"AREN'T YOU ALL GOING TO HIBERNATE?"
"US? YOU'RE JOKING!
THERE'S WORK TO BE DONE!"

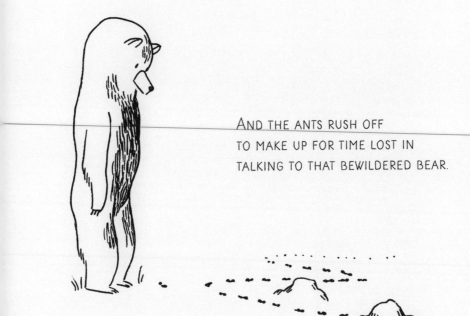

AND THE ANTS RUSH OFF
TO MAKE UP FOR TIME LOST IN
TALKING TO THAT BEWILDERED BEAR.

BJORN HESITATES, TOO,
WHEN HE MEETS THE CHICKADEE.
"IT IS TIME, ISN'T IT?"

"YES, BJORN, IT'S TIME.
THE SWALLOWS LEFT A LONG TIME AGO.
SO LONG AGO THAT NOW IT'S TIME."

"GOOD," HE SAYS TO HIMSELF.
AND HE SETS ABOUT HIS BEAR BUSINESS.

HE GATHERS APPLES.

HE MAKES SOME NICE HONEY
SANDWICHES WITHOUT BREAD.
HE CHOMPS DOWN WILD CARROTS,
SWALLOWS SOME EGGS THAT WERE
JUST LYING THERE.

SHARES DRIED FIGS WITH
THE BADGER.

HE CATCHES A BIG TROUT WITH A SINGLE SMACK
OF HIS PAW AND TOPS IT ALL OFF WITH A LARGE
FAT PAWFUL OF CHESTNUTS.

THEN HE CHECKS HIS BELLY FAT
AND RECKONS THAT YES, IT'LL DO.
THE SQUIRREL COMES BY.
HE AGREES THAT BJORN IS ALL SET.

THE RABBIT, CURIOUS,
HOPS UP AND OFFERS
HER OPINION: ALL SET.

THE FOX, WHO VERY MUCH LIKES TO BE CONSULTED,
INSPECTS BJORN, MAKES HIM TURN AROUND
A COUPLE OF TIMES, AND FINALLY DECLARES
THAT HE'S JUST RIGHT.

BJORN SMILES
AND YAWNS.

HE SCRATCHES HIMSELF
WITH HIS DELIGHTFUL FORK.

HE PUTS A BOOKMARK IN
THE MIDDLE OF THE CATALOGUES
HE'S BEEN READING.

He wishes all his friends a very pleasant winter and settles down comfortably, with a happy sigh, all the way at the back of his cave, setting his alarm clock for springtime.